Healthy Choices

Exercise and Rest

Sharon Dalgleish

Smart Apple Media

This edition first published in 2006 in the United States of America by Smart Apple Media.

Smart Apple Media
2140 Howard Drive West
North Mankato
Minnesota 56003

First published in 2006 by
MACMILLAN EDUCATION AUSTRALIA PTY LTD
627 Chapel Street, South Yarra, Australia 3141

Visit our Web site at www.macmillan.com.au

Associated companies and representatives throughout the world.

Library of Congress Cataloging-in-Publication Data

Dalgleish, Sharon.
   Exercise and rest / by Sharon Dalgleish.
     p. cm. -- (Healthy choices)
   Includes index.
   ISBN-13: 978-1-58340-755-4
   1. Exercise—Juvenile literature. 2. Rest--Juvenile literature. I. Title.

RA781.D32 2006
613.7'1—dc22

                      2005057878

Edited by Helen Bethune Moore
Text and cover design by Christine Deering
Page layout by Domenic Lauricella
Photo research by Legend Images
Illustrations by Paul Konye

Printed in USA

Acknowledgments
The author and the publisher are grateful to the following for permission to reproduce copyright material:

Front cover: Girls practising judo courtesy of Photolibrary/Photonica Inc.

Digital Vision, p. 21; The DW Stock Picture Library, pp. 14, 22; iStockphoto.com, p. 4 (left); Photodisc, pp. 6, 9 (centre), 24 (top & bottom), 26; Photolibrary/Agencie Images, p. 23; Photolibrary/Botanica, p. 11; Photolibrary/HTU/Science Photo Library, p. 25; Photolibrary/Index Stock Imagery, pp. 7, 8; Photolibrary/Mauritius Die Bildagentur Gmbh, p. 17; Photolibrary/Pacific Stock, p. 12; Photolibrary/Photonica Inc, pp. 1, 9 (left & right), 13, 18, 19; Photolibrary/Plainpicture Gmbh & Co. Kg, pp. 4 (centre), 30; Photolibrary/Reso E.E.I.G, pp. 3, 4 (right); Photolibrary/Leanne Temme, p. 10; Photolibrary/Veer, p. 27; Photolibrary/Workbook, Inc., p. 15.

While every care has been taken to trace and acknowledge copyright, the publisher tenders their apologies for any accidental infringement where copyright has proved untraceable. Where the attempt has been unsuccessful, the publisher welcomes information that would redress the situation.

Contents

Healthy, fit, and happy

To be healthy, fit, and happy your body needs:

- a good mix of foods
- plenty of clean drinking water
- a **balance** of activity and rest

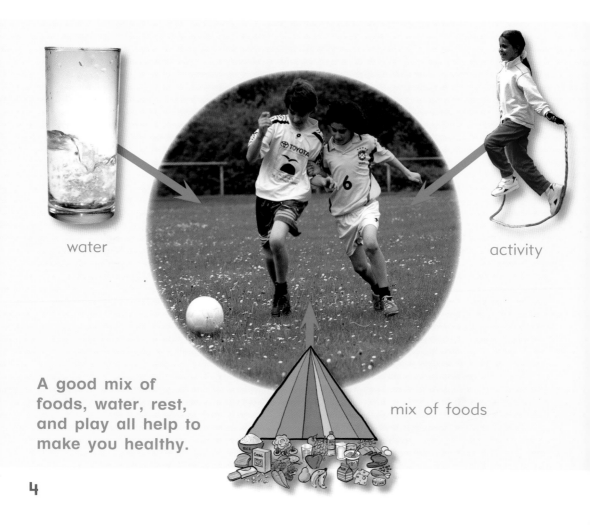

water

activity

A good mix of foods, water, rest, and play all help to make you healthy.

mix of foods

Active choices

It is important to make choices about what to eat to give you **energy**. It is important to make choices about which **activities** provide the exercise your body needs.

grains vegetables fruits oils dairy meat
                                foods and
                                       beans

The food group pyramid shows you which foods to eat most for a healthy, balanced diet.

Why make healthy choices?

Making healthy, active choices is important because your body is designed to move. If you are healthy, your body will feel good and work well.

If your body works well, you will have more energy for playing.

Watching TV, using the computer, or playing computer games are sit-down activities. The more time you spend doing them, the less time you have for being active.

It is good to stretch and move your body after playing computer games.

Healthy bones

Healthy bones need to move. Exercise makes the hard outside layer of your bones **dense**. Dense bones are tough. Weak bones can break with just a sneeze!

If your bones are not healthy they can break easily.

Daily exercise

You need at least 30 minutes of **moderate** exercise every day to make your bones dense. Do activities that make you puff, but not so puffed you cannot talk.

 +  +

10 minutes
walking

+

10 minutes
sliding

+

10 minutes bike riding

The 30 minutes of exercise does not have to be done all at once.

Activities you can do alone

There are plenty of things you can do to exercise by yourself. You could wash the family car, or invent a new dance.

Practice your skills on a hopscotch grid.

Being alone is the perfect time to practice something you want to get better at. You could practice hitting a tennis ball against a wall.

See how long you can twirl a hula hoop.

Activities to do with a friend

When a friend comes over, choose something active to do. If it is a hot day, remember to drink lots of water.

Wash the dog, then play a game with it.

If it is raining or cold outside, exercise inside. You could build a fort out of cardboard boxes, or have a dance competition.

Clapping games are a great way to stay active indoors.

Activities to do with your family

Adults need 30 minutes of activity every day, too. Help your whole family to make healthy choices by suggesting that you walk to the local shops, instead of driving.

If it is a short trip, leave the car at home and walk instead.

Whether your family is big or small, you can have fun being active together. Exercise is easy if everyone is having fun! You could go for a picnic.

If it snows where you live, you could make snow angels.

Healthy muscles

Healthy muscles need to be strong. You have over 600 muscles in your body. One or more of them help you every time you move, from blinking to cartwheeling.

When you bend your elbow, the biceps muscle shortens. This pulls your arm up.

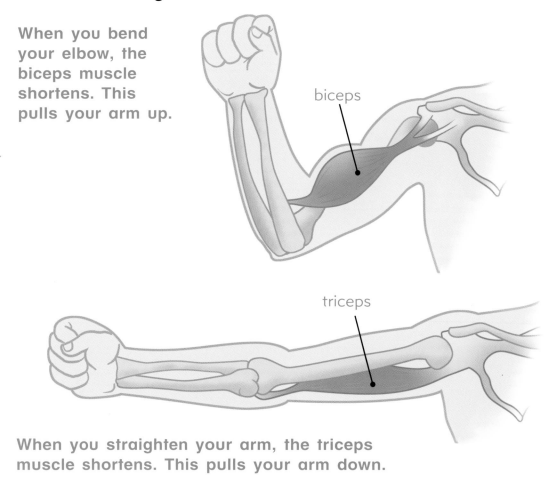

biceps

triceps

When you straighten your arm, the triceps muscle shortens. This pulls your arm down.

Test your arm strength

This test looks easy, but it is not! Try it to see how strong your arm muscles are.

What you need
- an open space
- a clock

What to do

1 Stand up and stretch out your arms at shoulder height. Make sure you are not touching anything.

2 See if you can keep your arms stretched out like this for five minutes. Your arms must stay at shoulder height the whole time.

Activities for fit muscles

Your muscles will stay strong and fit if you work them hard. Think of activities that make you feel powerful. These are the ones that build muscle strength.

Playing tug-of-war can make your muscles stronger.

Healthy muscles need to be **flexible**. This means they can bend and stretch and move easily. Activities that make you stretch make you flexible. They also feel good.

Healthy heart

You need a strong, healthy heart. It works hard all day and all night pumping blood around your body. It never stops to have a rest.

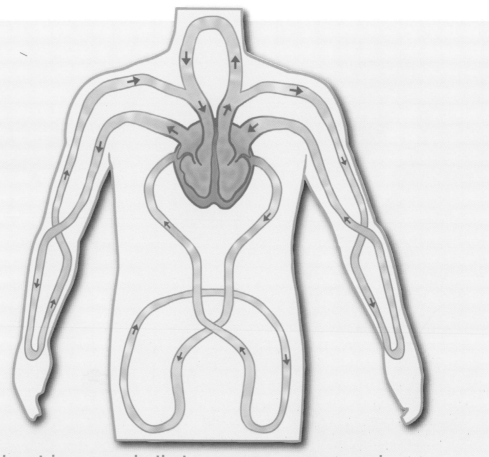

Your heart is a muscle that squeezes, pumps, and pushes your blood around your body.

Listen to your heartbeat

Your heart needs exercise, too. It should beat faster for at least 30 minutes three or four times a week. This is as well as the moderate activity you do every day.

What to do

1 Put your ear on a friend's chest and listen to the beat of their heart. A stethoscope helps, but you do not need one.
2 Ask your friend to jump up and down for five minutes.
3 Listen again. Is their heart beating faster?

Huff and puff activities

Activities that make you huff and puff make your heart pump faster. They are called **aerobic** exercises. They make you breathe faster than normal to get more air.

Aerobic activity can make you sweat, so drink lots of water.

Playing an active sport gets your heart pumping. Regular sports practice helps your heart get even better at its important job.

Active sports such as hockey or basketball are aerobic.

Food for exercise

Your body needs healthy food to get the energy to be active. Remember to eat a mix of different foods. Then you are more likely to get all the **nutrients** you need.

Playing with the dog or swimming is good exercise.

Healthy foods such as fruit, yogurt, and bread will give your body fuel for exercise.

The best drink to choose is fresh water. This is even more important when you are active. Remember to drink before, during, and after exercise.

Water is the best drink to stop you being thirsty.

Rest

You cannot be active all the time. Your body needs to take a break and rest. Sleeping is just as important as eating and exercising.

Every living creature needs sleep.

If you do not have enough sleep, you may not think clearly. You might do silly things. You may even get sick.

Sleep gives your body a chance to rest and repair itself.

Make a dream catcher

Native Americans make dream catchers so they can get a good night's rest. They believe the dream catcher traps bad dreams.

What you need
- a soft bendable twig, about 12 inches (30 centimeters) long
- tape
- string, about 3 feet (1 meter)
- beads with large holes
- feathers

What to do

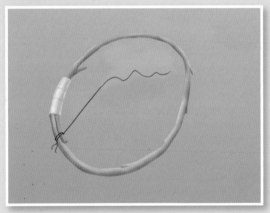

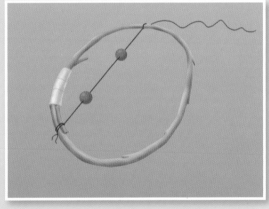

1 **Overlap the ends of the twig to make a hoop. Tape down the ends. Tie one end of string to the twig.**

2 **Knot the string and thread a bead onto it. Leave a few centimeters and repeat. Wrap the string around the other side of the hoop.**

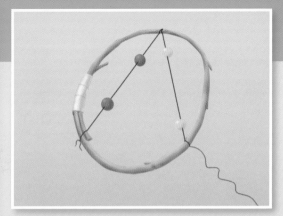

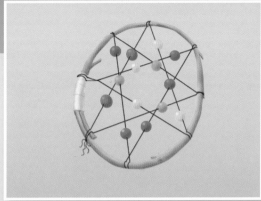

3 Thread two more beads onto the string. Wrap the string around the other side of the hoop.

4 Keep repeating until you have a web. Tie the end of the string onto the hoop at the same place you began.

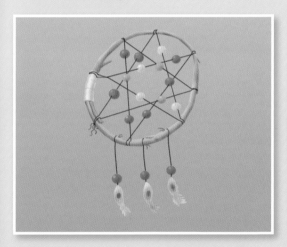

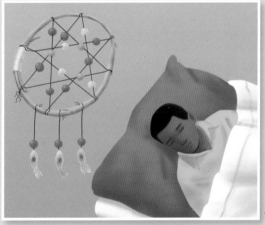

5 Tie three short lengths of string to the bottom of the hoop. Thread a bead onto each one and tie a feather to each end.

6 Hang your dream catcher near your bed.

29

Healthy choices for life

Making healthy choices in everything you do will help you to be fit, happy, and healthy.

Life is fun when you make healthy choices.

Glossary

activities	things that people do
aerobic	exercises that make you breathe faster
balance	an equal amount of different things
dense	thick
energy	strength to do things
flexible	able to move and bend easily
moderate	not too fast and not too slow
nutrients	healthy substances found in food, such as vitamins and minerals

Index